Shorty Bean
and the
Enchanted Coins

Seek and You Wi

by

Holly K. Szurpicki

Shorty Bean and the Enchanted Coins
Copyright © 2010—Holly K. Szurpicki

ISBN 978-0-9992323-1-6

Library of Congress Control Number: 2010900172
Szurpicki,H.K., 1976

Text Design: Lisa Simpson, Simpson Productions
Illustrations by Manneristic Studios

DaShawn L. Hall
NeKeysha Guyton- Art Director
Artistic contribution by:
Devon Bowers, Jenafer Cruz, Jetty Ann Kircher, Kieu Le,
Bethany Meier, Joseph Miller, Myrian Shipp, Derek Stewart,
Brian Thieme, Terry Valliere, Matt Wong, Nick Yarsulik

Front cover by Jenafer Cruz and Matt Wong
Back cover by Jenafer Cruz and NeKeysha Guyton

Dedication

To my amazing God and my husband for believing in me. To my two precious children, Jonathon and Colleen. To my mother, sister and grandfather and to all my darling nieces and nephews and especially Nana and Papa!

Special Thanks

DaShawn L. Hall and his marvelous team of talented artists from Manneristic Studios

Table of Contents

Seek and You Will Find

Life in the city is hectic and noisy, but in a tiny town up north where her grandparents live there is no notion of time for Shorty Bean and her beloved pet, Smarty. Together they discover a divine power that has been dormant for many years as they explore the Gazman Forest where they meet a bald eagle, an Indian chief, a blind cat, an anxious turtle, an Irish porcupine, a military fish and a royal frog.

But these discoveries are not without opposition as she encounters the winds of the north, the ravens of the air and the black bears.

This story is about a New World seen in the eyes of a little girl. A story of perseverance, family values, wonderful friends and divine destiny.

Join the adventures of the Shorty Bean series and discover an entire world filled with imagination that is just waiting for you to begin!

Chapter One

Daisy Toe Ring

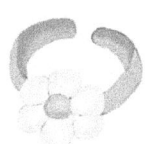

Everyone has something they like about themselves and for Shorty Bean it was her toes. She loved to display her white daisy toe ring and colorful toenails. Each time her mom bought her a new pair of tennis shoes, she immediately cut a hole in the top of her left shoe, so she could see her beloved daisy flower toe ring. But that wasn't all. She had a nail polish collection in every color of the rainbow and loved to paint each toenail in an array of assorted colors creating a rainbow of sorts on each foot.

Shorty Bean lived with her mom and dad in the big city. Where they lived there were lots of cars, people from different walks of life and lots of loud noises. The sounds of police sirens, ambulances, fire trucks and even car alarms often filled the air as she walked through the streets. Even though the city life sometimes drove her completely crazy, she loved it.

But, one of Shorty Bean's favorite places in the world was her grandparent's cottage up north. She would often daydream of their warm, yet simple home. Each time she did, a peaceful tranquility filled her heart and quieted her soul. If she was honest, she would have to admit she loved the quiet country far more than the busy city life.

Shorty Bean had an unusual looking pet named Smarty. He is what some people call a "mutt" which means no one exactly knew his pedigree. He was small and looked part dog and part hamster with a long black tail. His feet were not paws like a dog, but more like the small pads of a hamster's paw and his head, well that was a mix between the two. One might even call him a hamdog or something of that sort!

Smarty often wore brown aviation goggles that made his eyes look twice as big as they were. Most people, when they met him, thought he was a weird little rat. But Shorty Bean didn't feel that way about him at all for Smarty was her best friend.

Shorty Bean loved to sew things by hand. One day she made Smarty a red cape with patches. These weren't patches to mend a tear in the cape. No, they were for remembrances. Each time they did something special together, she sewed a new patch on to remember their adventure. So far, there were only a few patches on his red cape for it was still rather new and in the life of a little girl and her dog, that could change at any time.

Although Smarty couldn't talk, Shorty Bean and Smarty had no trouble communicating. They could communicate with sign language and could seem to read each other's thoughts by their facial expressions. One look would tell the story most of the time.

School was in session and it was always hard to leave him home alone for the day. But school was no place for a hamdog. The dreaded school bell rang. It was loud and hurt her ears. Although she hated the sound, it also meant the day was officially over and soon she would be homeward bound! Shorty Bean jumped up and down in her seat on the bus all the whole way home. She couldn't wait to see her best friend, Smarty.

"Mom, open the door!" Shorty Bean hollered as she knocked loudly on the front door.

"Hang on a minute, little lady!" her mom replied as she turned the latch and opened the door. "Well, how was your day at school?"

"It was an especially wonderful day. I got a 100% on my spelling test!" Shorty exclaimed with a sparkle in her eyes.

"You did! As always, I am so proud of you," her mother exclaimed as she wrapped Shorty in a hug. "I think your achievement deserves something really special. A night out perhaps?"

"Yeah, that is what I am talking about," Shorty Bean replied with a clap of her hands as she jumped up and down.

The phone rang. Shorty's mom walked into the kitchen to answer it as Shorty ran to get Smarty. As she did her mother's voice drifted through the house, "Hello Cattie, how are you?"

Shorty Bean's ears perked up at the name of her cousin Cattie. Cattie's mother, Aunt Flo, was her mother's only sister. Shorty Bean listened as the conversation continued.

"Mom is really sick," Cattie explained to Shorty Bean's mother. "Can you come?"

"Of course, honey!" she replied as Cattie informed her mother of Aunt Flo's symptoms and condition.

After a few minutes, her mom hung up the phone and bent her head to pray. She had much to do before heading to her sister's house.

A few hours later, Shorty Bean heard her Dad's car pull into the driveway. She ran to the front door and pulled it open to give him a big hug. "Dinner's ready, Dad!" she told him as she took his hand and guided him to the table. He sank into the chair.

"Long day?" Mom asked him as she sat in the chair next to him. He nodded, but smiled. Shorty Bean's dad was a hard worker.

"I received a call from Cattie," Shorty's mom began after they had prayed over the food. Flo is really ill again, and Cattie asked if I would be able to come and help care of her..." she stated as her voice trailed off. Lines of worry etched her forehead. Dad swiftly made the decision that Shorty Bean would go to Grandpa Andy's cottage in Cantina Village, a tiny town up north. With Dad working so many hours, they didn't want Shorty Bean to be all alone if her mother was gone. It made sense, but that didn't mean it would be easy.

"May I be excused?" Shorty Bean asked as her parents continued to discuss the situation. All of a sudden, she wasn't very hungry. She didn't want to leave her Mom and Dad and would miss them a whole bunch. She walked to her room and sat quietly in thought for a while. But then she realized that seeing her grandma and grandpa and the chance to go to her favorite cottage sounded like a great idea! She left her room in search of her Dad. She knew it was hard on her parent's as well. She found her dad sitting on the couch. Shorty Bean sat down beside him and laid her head on his lap.

Dad put one arm around her as he rubbed her head. It always comforted Shorty Bean to feel his arms around her.

"Dad, it's alright with me," Shorty Bean began. "I would love to see Grandma and Grandpa."

"I am glad, Shorty Bean," Dad replied. "And they would love to see you, too. But, you look like you are getting sleepy. What do you say we call it a night and I will tuck you into bed?" Dad asked.

"Yes, I am ready for bed," Shorty Bean replied with a yawn. She and her Dad walked upstairs to her bedroom and she hopped up on her covers. Smarty jumped up right next to her. Suddenly Dad yelled, "Get that rat out of your bed!"

"Daddy, you know Smarty always sleeps with me," Shorty Bean replied with surprise.

"You are not supposed to have animals in your bed!" Dad exclaimed. "And why do you make him wear that ridiculous cape, anyway?"

"Dad, please, pretty please, just until I fall asleep?" she begged.

"Alright," he responded. "But know this, if I come in here in the morning and that rat, hamster, hamdog or whatever it is, is on your bed again, then that's it. He's going to be living outside!"

Shorty Bean gave a small nod to her dad as he walked out. She looked down at Smarty and signed a heart to him. He laid his paw on her shoulder as he snuggled next to her. Within no time at all, the sounds of snoring fill the air. ZZZZZ...ZZZZZZ. From Smarty, that is.

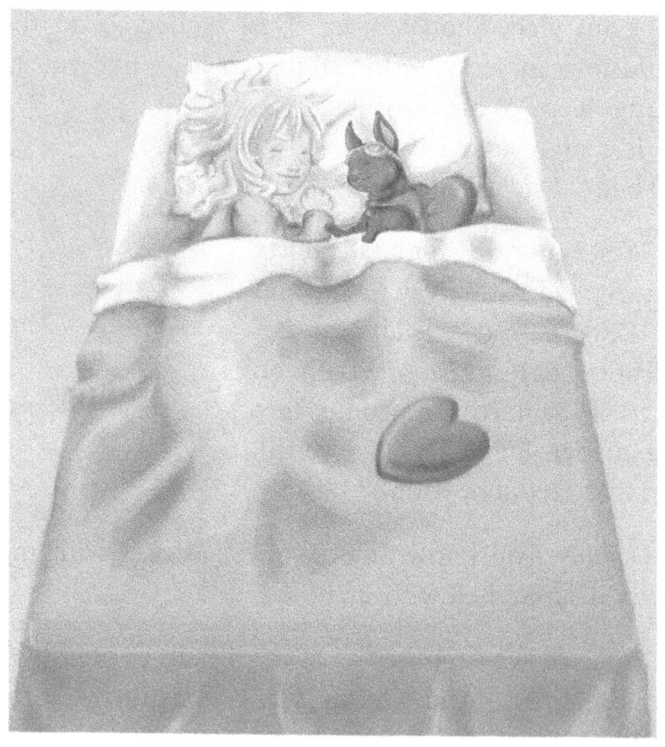

Chapter Two

Road Trip

L ight peeked through the curtains of Shorty Bean's room. She didn't remember when she finally fell asleep, but her tired body protested as she started to get up. She pulled out her small suitcase from under her bed and began to pack to go to her grandparent's cottage. She gathered up all her clothes, shoes, hairclips, and brushes. And she couldn't forget her collection of nail polish and glitter lip-gloss—a must for every girl!

Smarty, who was still on the bed, crawled over near her dresser. He grabbed his extra pair of goggles for Shorty Bean to pack for him. "Oh, thank you, Smarty! I might have forgotten those!" she said as she rubbed his back. She double checked her belongings in the suitcase then clicked the lid shut.

"Hurry, Shorty Bean. We need to go. I'll wait for you in the car," her dad yelled from downstairs. Shorty Bean hustled down the stairs, but stopped at the front door. She almost forgot her hat, her backpack and her coat! She quickly grabbed her backpack and slung it over her shoulder as she carried her coat and hat in one hand and her suitcase in the other. "Come on, Smarty. It's time to go." She shut the door behind her until she heard it click. She wondered how long it would be before she would be home again.

Her mom was waiting beside the car to give her a hug. She had been up late packing her own suitcase and preparing to leave for Aunt Flo's. Shorty Bean threw her arms around her mom and hung on. Tears flowed from

her deep blue eyes. Ah, the love between a mother and a daughter is precious.

"You won't have to stay at Grandpa Andy's and Grandma Ellie's very long. I promise," her mom spoke into her ear as she held her close. She pulled away slightly and wiped the tears from Shorty Bean's cheeks. "I love you and will see you soon! Now hurry and get in the car," her mom said as she opened the passenger door for her.

"Come on Shorty Bean. We need to hustle," her dad commented as he put the car in reverse. Shorty saw her mom blow them both lots of kisses as they pulled out of the driveway. Almost immediately Smarty jumped from the back seat onto Shorty Bean's lap.

"Can I ask you this question? Why are you bringing that rat?" Dad asked.

"Dad, he's not a rat! And I can't leave him all alone! Who would give him water or rub his little head?" Shorty Bean replied as she tucked her arm around her friend.

"Well keep him in your backpack during the trip," her dad responded. Shorty Bean's dad and Smarty were not close at all. At least not yet. But Shorty Bean was determined that one day they would be.

"Alright," Shorty Bean agreed with a sigh. She zipped open her backpack and carefully placed Smarty on a small towel she kept inside for just such an occasion. "It's okay, Smarty. Go to sleep. We will be there soon, and I can take you out," she told him as she zipped the pouch closed, but not all the way so he could breathe.

In no time her father had turned onto the interstate freeway towards Grandpa Andy's and Grandma Ellie's cottage. Shorty Bean settled into her seat and stared at the scenery as it whizzed by. She loved traveling to her grandparents' cottage. It would take about an hour or so to get out of the city limits, but then it was like entering another world. The air smelled quite different and she took a deep breath to let it fill her lungs as peace settled into her soul.

The loud sounds of the city gave way to the quietness of the countryside. Shorty Bean peered out the car window at the acres of pine trees that filled the forests beyond the road. Smarty poked his head out of the backpack. He was curious to see them also. Varying hues of both gold and dark green blended together beautifully. She glimpsed at the majestic pines towering high above them. Rays of sunlight danced throughout the clouds touching the very tops of the trees giving them a heavenly glow.

"Aren't they beautiful, Dad?" Shorty Bean exclaimed. She never got tired of looking at them.

"Yes, they are quite majestic, I agree, Shorty Bean," her dad responded as he took a quick glance away from the road. "You know once outside the city limits and away from the pollution, the sun can shine through with greater clarity and everything looks clearer and cleaner. The farther north you travel the less air pollutants there are."

Shorty nodded at his statement. "Are we almost there?" she asked.

Her dad chuckled. "I was wondering when you were going to ask me that! Yes, we have about ten more miles, Shorty."

"Dad, do you think we can stop at the little store and get a grape soda?" she asked in anticipation. There was always something special about heading to Grandma and Grandpa's and stopping at the store was one of them.

"Sure, I don't see why not. Mouse and Mats Party store is right up the road," he replied.

Smarty smiled. Her favorite part was picking out grape soda out of the barrel that was filled with crushed ice. Smarty was excited too and his tongue was hanging out in anticipation.

As the stored came into view, they pulled over. Her dad first filled up the tank with gasoline. As he did, Shorty Bean and Smarty, (she had pulled out of the backpack for the short break and now held him in her hand) started to window shop at the little gift store attached to the party store.

Once inside, Shorty Bean discovered a seashell mirror with a red velvet backing. She adored the mirror.

"Dad, will you buy it for me?" she asked with pleading eyes when he came inside. "Please?"

"I never could resist those eyes. How much is it?" he asked.

An inexpensive item, he nodded his head and handed Shorty the money to purchase the small mirror. She beamed as she tucked it away in a small side pocket of the backpack as they climbed back into the car to finish the trip. Shorty was content sipping her soda. She couldn't wait to see her grandparents, it wouldn't be long now.

Smarty watched her intently hoping to catch a drop of the purple drink. Grape soda was also his favorite flavor.

They turned off the highway and the paved road turned onto dirt signaling they were close. This was real country living, but it also had its challenges as the dirt roads often were pitted with the occasional pot hole. Each time it rained, the water washed away part of the dirt from the surface of the road until small holes formed. Shorty Bean loved dirt roads with big old potholes. About every couple of minutes or so, Dad would hit one and the car would jump. Up and down, up and down, it was like a mini roller coaster ride.

"Hang on!" he stated as they hit a particularly big one that he couldn't dodge. Shorty Bean laughed to herself as she glanced at her Dad. His knuckles were white as they gripped the steering wheel and perspiration beaded on his forehead. Dad always worried that the car frame would fall apart with each new hole he ran over. But for Shorty and Smarty, it was a fun ride.

Chapter Three

The Cottage

Not long afterwards, they pulled into the circular driveway of her grandparent's cottage. White smoke rose from the chimney that meant a cozy fire in the fireplace. Shorty Bean loved fall, the cool breeze, the changing colors and especially the leaves falling from the trees. She climbed out of the car and turned in a circle through the leaves that had fallen to the ground. A gentle breeze swept them in waves to wherever their new homes would be.

Shorty Bean grabbed her belongings and started toward the cottage where she saw Grandma Ellie and Grandpa Andy's two favorite white rocking chairs on the big covered front porch. The cottage was barn red, her favorite color, and had heart shaped white shutters and bright yellow flowers in window boxes under each window. Before she could reach the porch, Grandpa opened the front screen door to greet them. The smell of homemade biscuits filled the air. Instantly she realized how much she had missed her grandparents and being up north in this beautiful place.

Grandpa walked down the steps and gave Shorty a huge hug. Then he stepped back, put his hands on his overall straps, and looked her over with a big grin "Shorty Bean, you are getting so big! Now go on and see your Grandma. She is in the kitchen cookin' away some of your favorites," he said.

Shorty Bean ran inside as the screen door slammed behind her. She couldn't wait to see Grandma Ellie. Meanwhile, Grandpa and Dad sat down in the two white rockers on the porch and talked about Aunt Flo. Both were concerned that she might not live much longer.

"Grandma! Grandma!" Shorty cried out as she burst into the kitchen.

"Hello, my dear. Look at you! Every time I see you, you look more and more like your mother," Grandma Ellie exclaimed. "Come, my dear and sit down. I just took some biscuits out of the oven. They are still very warm," Grandma said as she pulled some blackberry honey from the pantry and sat it next to the plate of biscuits. "Would you like some honey?" she asked.

"Absolutely!" Shorty replied. Shorty Bean could not wait! She placed her backpack under the kitchen table and sat down in her favorite old painted wooden chair. Grandma took the warm biscuits and piled them with mound of blackberry honey. She gave Shorty a cup of hot tea with milk. "Mmmmm," Shorty said with a mouth full of biscuit as some honey dripped onto her shoe.

Just them Smarty stuck his head out of the open backpack, his nose twitching in the air. He climbed out and up Shorty's leg to try to lick the honey from her shoes.

"Smarty, that tickles!" Shorty Bean laughed as she picked him up and placed him in her lap.

"Would you like some more tea and milk?" Grandma Ellie asked.

"Yes, Grandma that would be great," Shorty Bean replied. "I would love some more."

Shorty watched as her grandma poured the steaming liquid into her mug. It warmed her hands as she held the cup. She poured some milk in and stirred it to cool the drink. As soon as Grandma Ellie turned around to clean the kitchen counters, Shorty Bean quietly moved her tea cup under the table for Smarty. He needed to have a little bit to drink too! A smile crossed Grandma Ellie's face as she continued to wipe the counters. Not much escaped her notice, even if Shorty thought it did!

Once Smarty was finished with his drink, Shorty put her index finger over her lips to indicate the need for quiet. Smarty understood and crawled back into the backpack. Once inside he poked his head out to see if the coast was clear. Shorty giggled at the sight for all you could see was his goggles and his big observant, hazel eyes.

Just then, Dad strolled into the kitchen where they were and sat down next to Shorty. "I have to go now," he said as he squeezed her hand. "I want you to promise me that you will be good for your grandpa and grandma, and you will keep that rat out of trouble! I love you very much! I will be back to get you as soon as I can," he finished.

As he stood to leave, Shorty Bean reached up and put her arms around his neck. "I love you, too Dad," she replied as she gave him a big hug and a kiss on his cheek. Grandpa Andy and Grandma Ellie joined them as they walked with him out to the porch. They watched and waved from the two white rocking chairs where Shorty Bean and Grandpa Andy now sat while her dad pulled out and sped away.

"Would you like to go and see my new garden out back?" he asked.

"Sure" she replied, she thought that was a great idea.

When Grandma Ellie was not looking, Smarty slipped out from the backpack and ran to the front porch. Shorty scooped him up in her hand as she and Grandpa Andy decided to take a walk to see the new garden.

Shorty held her grandfather's hand with one hand and with the other kept Smarty tucked into her arm as they walked through the grass to the garden behind the house. After riding in the car for a while, it was nice to stretch her legs. She breathed in the fresh air and was completely relaxed. With her best friend in her arms and her grandpa by her side, this certainly would be a great adventure.

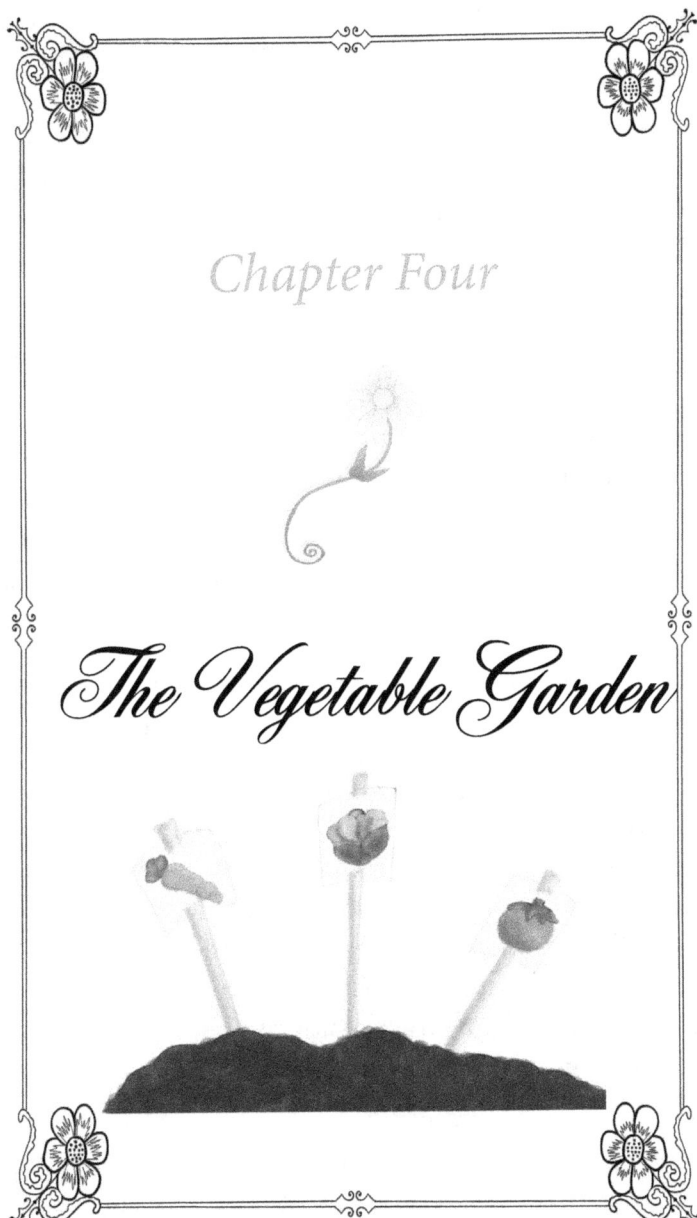

Chapter Four

The Vegetable Garden

While Grandpa Andy and Shorty Bean walked through the garden, Grandma Ellie yelled out to them from the kitchen window. "Andy, can you pick me some lettuce, carrots and tomatoes from the garden, will yaw? Pretty please!" Grandma Ellie added with a laugh. "Yes, Ma'am!" Grandpa replied. Grandpa Andy let Shorty Bean pick some vegetables from the garden plants. She headed over near the cucumbers to pick some tomatoes, "Don't pick the green ones. They are not ripe yet," he instructed.

Shorty searched for the reddest ones she could find. Grandpa Andy came over to observe her.

"That's a perfect choice!" he exclaimed. Now put them here in this basket. Let's see, did we get everything your grandma requested?"

"Yes, I believe we did, Grandpa," Shorty Bean replied. Grandpa Andy and Shorty turned to go back to the cottage with their baskets filled with vegetables

"Why, thank you!" Grandma Ellie said as she took the basket of vegetables from Shorty. "These look wonderful!" Shorty signed to Smarty and he jumped back inside the backpack. They returned to the kitchen to help grandma clean and wash the vegetables. The water in the sink turned a light brown color as they washed them. Shorty realized there can be a lot of dirt that collects on the vegetables as they grow.

"You must clean them before you can eat them," Grandma Ellie instructed as they finished rinsing the vegetables. She was preparing a salad for their dinner. Shorty Bean loved salad. It was one of her favorite foods!

The delicious smells from the food cooking on the stove, combined with the gentle hum of the running water and the warm kitchen made Shorty quite sleepy. She yawned and so did Smarty. They had gotten up earlier than usual to make the trip. "Can I go lay on the couch and listen to Grandpa Andy's old vinyl records, grandma?" She asked.

"Of course you can, honey. I can finish the rest myself. You go rest," Grandma Ellie assured her.

Shorty Bean grabbed Smarty and went to the couch to relax and listen. Grandpa Andy's records were from artists that were before her time. They were from the 1920s through the 1950s. As she listened to the old melodies, it would quiet her spirit. Before she knew it, she heard her grandmother's voice "Dinner time!" as the dinner bell from the porch rang loudly. It startled her awake.

"Now, that is what I am talking about," Shorty Bean said to herself as she jumped up off the couch. She headed to the dining room and sat down as she waited for Grandma Ellie to pass her plate. Yum! Vegetables and salad greens were two of her favorite foods and Grandma Ellie always made sure she had plenty of them. She closed her eyes and chewed slowly savoring the taste, "Mmmmm!" she exclaimed after almost every bite.

"That was great Grandma! My stomach is so full it might just blow up!" Shorty said with laughter. "After we finish the dishes, do you think I could turn into bed a little early tonight? I am so tired!"

Grandma Ellie patted Shorty Bean on her head, "Sure love. You can go on up to bed now. When I am finished cleaning up the kitchen, I will come upstairs and tuck you and Smarty into bed."

"Alright Grandma, I love you." Shorty Bean replied as she turned to walk up the stairs to her room. As she walked down the hallway she smelled the familiar scent of lavender which always filled her grandparent's home. She glanced at the old photos in picture frames along the wall until she reached her room. On the door was a little sign that read "For our humble guest."

Inside, the curtains on the windows were long and pure white in color. The bed was soft and feathery with pink blankets and two pink full-size feather down pillows. The room had the same smell of lavender from the flowers that had been placed in tiny sterling silver antique vases which Grandma Ellie collected over the years.

This was no ordinary place. Deep in the forest were all kinds of creatures and Shorty Bean understood them just like she did Smarty. There were no limits to her imagination.

Chapter Five

Goodnight, Shorty Bean

Grandma Ellie walked up the stairs to Shorty Bean's bedroom. When Shorty heard her footsteps, she quickly hopped into bed. Grandma never missed an opportunity to tuck her granddaughter in bed for the night. Grandma Ellie pulled the blankets up over her and tucked her in snug. Then she knelt on her knees beside Shorty's bed and began to pray.

"As night falls and the sky begins to sleep, I pray the Lord your soul to keep. I know that angels will be sitting nearby, to watch you at night and fly, fly, fly. Snuggle in bed, my dear, and dream of candy canes and elephant ears. Think about what daybreak will bring, as we wake to another day and sing. Bless the skies, the oceans, the seasons and the sun. Bless mommies and daddies and little girls too, and Smarties and grandpas and grandmas too. And help us to always remember You, You, You. Amen," grandma finished as she bent down to kiss Shorty on the forehead.

"Goodnight, Grandma." Shorty Bean smiled ever so pleasantly.

"Goodnight, Shorty Bean. I love you so very much," Grandma responded as she gently stroked Shorty's head. "And goodnight to you too, Mr. Smarty," she said as Smarty curled up next to Shorty. He waved goodnight and then took his tiny little paws and laid them on Shorty Bean's pillow near her head. Grandma Ellie turned out the light and quietly closed the bedroom door. Curled up in the covers, Shorty Bean took a deep breath. The last thing she remembered was the fresh scent of the lavender before she fell fast asleep.

Bang! Shorty Bean's eyes flew open. What happened? Her window was open and the cold air blew into the room and through her hair. Brrr! Shorty Bean jumped out of bed to close the window. As she stared out into the inky darkness, she noticed a path of lights glowing through the pine trees. It was mysterious, and she wondered where it could possibly lead. Never one to miss out on an adventure, Shorty Bean quickly woke Smarty and motioned for him to get his coat on and follow her. Smarty was so tired and wasn't sure he wanted to leave the warmth of the cozy blankets. He ducked his head back under the covers. Shorty walked over to the bed and tapped the top of his head under the blanket. "Smarty get up! Come on! I will give you a blanket and you can hide in my backpack if you go with me," she begged.

With a deep sigh, Smarty crawled out of the warmth to get his coat as Shorty Bean pulled on her tennis shoes, which of course had the toes cut out, so she could see her toe ring. She wiggled her toes, looked at her toe ring and smiled before grabbing her coat and hat. Next, she picked up Smarty and placed him on one shoulder as she slung her backpack on the other.

Shorty tiptoed to the bedroom door and quietly opened it. She paused to listen until she was confident that all was still. Then slowly she crept down the stairs careful where she placed her feet. In an old cottage, the floorboards often creak. Shorty Bean was worried that the sound of the creaking wood floor might wake Grandma Ellie and Grandpa Andy who were sleeping in a bedroom just below her. She made it down the stairs, glided past their room and straight to the back door.

As Shorty stepped out onto the back porch, a shadowy object emerged from underneath the backyard deck. It was a cat.

"Who goes there?" the cat asked while banging her guide stick on the ground. As her eyes adjusted to the darkness Shorty Bean recognized who it was.

"Well, if it isn't the blind old cat, Mrs. Patty," Shorty exclaimed. Mrs. Patty did not live in the forest, but you couldn't get to it without passing through her first.

"What are you doing up so late, Shorty Bean?" asked Mrs. Patty. Shorty Bean motioned for Smarty to be quiet. He had a habit of making high pitched noises when he wasn't suppose to and she didn't want to wake her grandparents.

Mrs. Patty was an old blind cat who loved to dress up in flowered dresses in vivid colors along with old stylish hats adorned with wild flowers she had picked from the woods nearby. She sometimes even wore pink curlers in her fur and red and green fabric scarves.

"How do I look, and what do you think of my new hat?" Mrs. Patty asked. Each time Shorty saw Mrs. Patty, the blind cat would ask how she looked. Shorty could never understand why it mattered since she was unable to see herself, but nevertheless, remembered that everyone likes to hear compliments now and then.

"Shhh! Please whisper, Mrs. Patty. I do not want to wake Grandma and Grandpa," Shorty Bean responded with her index finger up to her mouth before she continued. "I just love your outfit. It matches your dress perfectly and looks just amazing with the color of your eyes." Shorty Bean chuckled.

Mrs. Patty smiled. "Thank you dear. I do think so myself. Now the two of you hurry back and don't be gone for too long," Mrs. Patty instructed as she stumbled slightly in her effort to get back under the deck. A small thud indicated she had hit her head on the door of her home. It was amazing she could get around as well as she did being blind and all. "Are you alright?" Shorty asked as she stepped down off the porch concerned for her friend. Mrs. Patty didn't even care about bumping her head. She was more concerned with how she looked. What a silly cat she was!

Mrs. Patty just chuckled, "Certainly, my dear, but could you tell me, is my hat on, right?"

Shorty quickly adjusted the hat tipping it slightly forward and smiled. "Yes, it is," she replied "Goodnight, Mrs. Patty," Shorty said with a wave as she and Smarty started toward the woods in search of the mysterious path of lights. The wind started to pick up as they walked toward the lights. There was no way she or Smarty would have ever guessed what they were about to find.

Chapter Six

The Divine Discovery

S horty Bean's eyes grew wide as she skipped down to the pathway of lights which were actually pickling jars bursting full of fireflies. Their little bug bodies were buzzing around inside the pickling jars which gave off a glistening green glow. Without warning, dirt started to blow in her face as a sudden gust of wind swept through and circled around her. It was almost like a mini tornado. Smarty popped his head up through the top of her backpack, but the wind was blowing too hard, so he ducked his head back in. Shorty heard him sneeze and felt the backpack quiver. "Calm down Smarty," Shorty Bean said. "Everything will be alright. It's just a storm."

Shorty Bean blinked because of the dirt that had blown into her eyes. Suddenly, it grew completely still. It was almost eerie it was so quiet. Shorty opened her eyes. Immediately she glanced at her toes to make sure her daisy toe ring was still there. Then she noticed a copper tin box out of the corner of her eye.

She bent down to the ground and swept the dust away from the top of the box. It was a decent size, but it appeared to be sunk deep into the ground. She tried to pull it out. With a couple of strong tugs from each side, it broke free. Once out of the ground, she blew the rest of the dirt from the top of the box, revealing five words, "Seek and you will find."

Shorty Bean was curious about what was inside the box, but she didn't want to pick it up right away. She was afraid she may disturb its contents. It was too dark to see inside, so she decided to drag the box over to the firefly jars for some extra light.

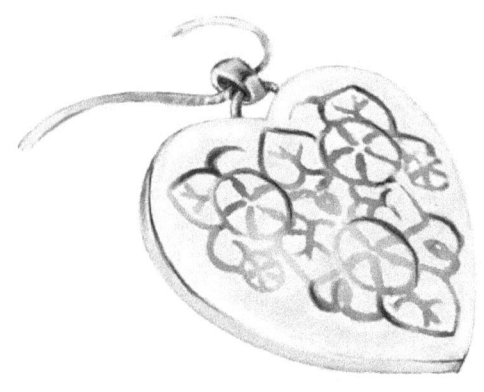

That was better. She reached inside and pulled out a gold heart-shaped locket necklace. It was beautiful. It had a pattern edged on the outside which looked like flowers that she had seen before. Immediately she opened the locket. A brilliant light radiated from inside where there were four chambers. Each chamber held what looked like a placeholder for a small coin. The coin was missing, but an illustration of the coin remained.

Shorty studied each illustration separately. The coin of the first chamber was of a soaring white dove. The second chamber's coin was of a pounding crimson heart. The third chamber's coin was of a powerful, gusting wind. The coin in the fourth chamber revealed flames of fire radiating with a warm orange illumination. Shorty looked at Smarty. Both of their eyes were as big as saucers.

Suddenly, a piece of scrolled paper appeared right in front of them. Shorty Bean picked it up and unrolled it next to the fireflies' jar for light. The mysterious letter was addressed to her!

"Shorty Bean, only you can unleash the secrets that lay at rest in this locket. The time has come for you to journey through the Gazman Forest where you must find the actual enchanted coins you have seen pictured in the locket. Each coin must be placed in its own chamber of power. No other eye can view this secret mystery but yours. This treasure box and the coins contained therein were not destined for merely anyone to behold. Only those who cherish the gift of imagination can truly understand this secret mystery. You, Shorty Bean, and your furry friend qualify.

Through the forest, you will meet friends. Each is important and will help you find each golden coin of power. Ben-Jeer is a royal frog who lives in the lily pads of Thunder Rail Lake among the lady slippers. Sir Davy is a Civil War fish who is the commander of the Little Dix River. Tripod, the defender of the box turtles, will lead you to the sun which is White Cloud. He will hold the last coin of the locket—the coin of fire. But, there is also an evil that will seek you out for the power that rests upon each coin. You must beware of the evil black bears, the ravens and the northern winds. They will not be able to harm you if you hold the locket and the protection it possesses. Look for Ms. Nora. She is waiting for you in a tree outside of Nussle Ridge Creek.

You must look beyond the chambers of this locket with your faith to unleash a treasure map that will help guide you on your journey. Finally, keep this locket around your neck and hold it dear to your heart. It is your protection and your destiny.

Shorty Bean, you have been predestined to find these enchanted coins. The locket will be complete only when all the gold coins are found and placed within their chambers. Then the mystery of the enchanted coins will be revealed to you. Follow the locket and be strong."

Once Shorty Bean had finished reading each word, it was consumed by fire. When she was done, all that was left was a pile of ashes that blew away into the darkness as a voice rumbled, "Seek and you will find" and then all grew quiet.

Shorty Bean's hands were shaking as she picked up the locket. She clasped it securely around her neck on the third try. She tucked Smarty safely in her backpack and took a deep breath. What did it all mean? The glow of the fireflies had dimmed, and the pathway was now very dark. Shorty looked around as the wind picked back up and blew her hair around her face. She pulled her coat close as the north wind cut threw her. She ran as fast as she could towards the cottage.

Once she reached the deck she was out of breath. She bent over with her hands on her knees to rest when suddenly a loud THUMP! THUMP! could be heard and felt under her feet. Shorty jumped and with heart racing peered through the dark cracks of the decking. It was only Mrs. Patty. She had bumped into one of the posts under the deck! She stood in front of her oval mirror as she changed her hat. "How do I look?" she asked.

"Great! Goodnight!" Shorty Bean said with a nervous laugh. She did not have time for small chatter with Mrs. Patty. She quietly ran upstairs to her bedroom. She threw her coat and shoes on the floor, grabbed Smarty from the backpack and jumped into bed pulling the covers over her head. It was going to be hard to fall sleep after everything that just happened, but Shorty was determined.

Chapter Seven

Just Believe

The smell of homemade biscuits and Grandma Ellie's singing rose up from the kitchen and woke Shorty Bean from her short night of sleep. She jumped out of bed and ran down the stairs. "Grandma, Grandma, I found a treasure in the garden last night!"

"You did?" Grandma exclaimed. "What were you doing outside in the middle of the night?"

"Well," she paused slightly before continuing, "I woke up when a strong wind blew my window open and then I saw a lighted path in the forest. It was hard to resist its glow. So, Smarty and I went to see what it was. We found a copper box, a locket and a letter!" Shorty Bean exclaimed trying to catch her breath.

"Really, you don't say?" Grandma Ellie replied with an amused look. "Grandpa Andy, come here and listen to what your granddaughter is saying."

"Wait! I am serious! Listen to me!" Shorty Bean almost shouted. "Grandpa, I went into the garden last night."

"You mean the vegetable garden?" Grandpa questioned. "Slow down, breathe slowly and relax, Shorty Bean."

"No Grandpa, the garden in the forest with the fireflies. There was a line of pickling jars—full of them—they were lighting the pathway," she explained.

"Those old jars? Honey, all they are full of is dead bugs!" he said with a chuckle. "So, tell me, what did you find?" he asked

"I found a treasure—a golden locket. Here, go on, take a look at it," she insisted as she reached into her pocket and pulled it out for him to see.

Grandpa Andy turned it over gently in his hand. "This locket looks quite old and it seems to be in pretty poor condition." He carefully opened the latch. "Too bad it's empty. Just some dirt inside is all."

"Empty? No, it is certainly not!" Shorty Bean exclaimed as she reached for the locket. "There is a dove soaring and a heart beating and wind and fire. There is even a treasure map," she explained.

"Okay, whatever you say," Grandpa Andy said going along with Shorty Bean. He thought it was all a make-believe story and was certainly willing to play along.

"Grandpa, I am telling the truth!" Shorty insisted. "Don't you believe me?"

"Yes, I do believe you, Shorty, but sometimes in life, we don't all see things in the same way that is all. It does not mean I don't believe you. If you said you saw it, then I believe that you did indeed!" he said kindly.

Shorty realized her grandfather truly couldn't see the illustrations inside the locket or the place for the missing coins. Her mind raced as she pondered. What had the scroll instructed?

"Grandpa, I have to go to see Ms. Nora. She lives in Nussle Ridge Creek. Do you know where I can find her?" Shorty asked.

"You know Shorty Bean, with your imagination, maybe you could ask the roses where to find her," Grandpa laughed as he tossed her hair. "I am sure they would tell you." Grandpa sipped his tea, winked at Grandma Ellie and smiled. But Shorty Bean knew what she had to do next.

As soon as she finished eating breakfast, Shorty Bean and Smarty did exactly what her grandfather had suggested and marched outside to the rose garden.

Chapter Eight

The Purple Rose

The sky was a deep blue and the sun was already well up in the sky when Shorty and Smarty entered the rose garden which was located not too far from the cottage. They followed the petite white fencing towards the back of the property several hundred yards before Shorty's eyes saw the most stunning rose garden. It seemed like a hundred vibrant colors exploded from the garden and sparkled like precious stones with hues of blue sapphires, orange topazes, white pearls, green emeralds and purple amethysts. They resembled a multi-colored rainbow. Shorty Bean decided to run back to the cottage. "Grandpa, will you go with me to the rose garden? Please, please," she begged.

"Yes, I will," he replied, but let me go get my rubber boots on and grab the rose clippers first." In a few minutes the three had started on the path to the rose garden, Grandpa Andy and Shorty holding hands as Smarty perched on Shorty's shoulder.

Grandpa Andy's words continued to roll through her mind as they walked toward the rose garden. Maybe he was right, and the roses could tell her where to find Mrs. Nora! But how could she ask a rose to explain to her where to go? Roses couldn't speak, or could they?

Shorty was still pondering that question as they walked into the garden. "Weeds; it never fails. No matter how many I pull up, there are always more," Grandpa stated almost to himself. "And they strangle my roses. If you want to keep your roses beautiful and growing strong, you must cut the weeds off them," he instructed

as he bent down to carefully clip out an unwelcome vine. "You must be careful to only cut the weeds, or you could destroy the beautiful rose," he explained as he cut and pruned.

He was so absorbed in his instruction to Shorty, Grandpa Andy accidentally snipped his finger with the clippers. Blood dripped from the wound.

"Ouch!" he yelped as he grabbed the hurt finger.

"Oh no! Grandpa, what happened?" Shorty Bean exclaimed.

"Listen, I have to go back to the cottage to bandage this up. It won't take but a minute. Just sit right here and wait for me, okay? I will be right back." While Grandpa trotted back to the cottage, Shorty sat in the garden as her Grandpa had asked. She was enjoying the beauty of the roses and decided to lay down on the ground. She put her hands behind her head to form a pillow and looked off at the clouds. The warmth of the sun beat down on her face and Shorty Bean closed her eyes and breathed in the sweet aroma of the roses. When she looked back at the sky, all the clouds had transformed into shapes! There was a sheep, cats, birds, chocolate candies, cotton candy, and all sorts of magnificent things.

Then she heard a beautiful voice, like a bell, calling her name, "Shorty! Shorty Bean!"

"Who is calling my name?" Shorty asked as she stood to her feet. She glanced around the garden, but there was no one there except herself and Smarty. Who could it be?

The voice grew louder, "Shorty! Shorty Bean! Look! Over here," the voice beckoned.

Shorty turned her head in the direction of the voice toward a beautiful purple rose. It was the rose talking to her! Just as she was about to speak, the amethyst rose, which was swaying in the soft wind, spoke gently, "You must go to see Ms. Nora."

Shorty Bean was amazed. "It's true! It is so true! You really are talking to me," Smarty said in awe.

The purple rose spoke again," You must go and see Ms. Nora, Shorty Bean. Just follow the pearl roses until you see one ruby rose. Then turn by the sycamore tree and stay on the path of hollow ferns. They will wind along the path and lead you to Nussle Creek Ridge. There under a tree you will find Ms. Nora." Once the purple rose finished speaking, its petals dropped off and swirled into the sky until they completely disappeared from her sight.

Shorty Bean held the locket tightly and positioned her backpack, with Smarty inside, securely on her back. She then continued down the pathway in hopes that she would find Ms. Nora.

Chapter Nine

Nussle Ridge Creek

Shorty Bean rehearsed the instructions she had received from the purple rose as she walked. "Okay, Smarty, what did she tell us next? Oh yes, follow the pearl roses until we find the ruby rose, turn at the sycamore tree and then follow the hollow ferns." It was a good thing Shorty Bean knew how to navigate through the forest. Her grandfather had made sure of that when they would take walks and he would instruct Shorty on the variety of trees. Once at the sycamore, they turned and continued down the path of ferns. But the path was beginning to disappear as the ferns increased and over-powered the pathway. Shorty could barely pick her way through them.

She opened the locket and looked behind the chamber. Perhaps it could help her. As she looked at the map, a sparkling color show of lights flickered and illuminated the location of the ruby rose. She took her finger and traced the line on the map until she came to a green hat lantern. A little further past the lantern, Shorty saw the tree.

"This must be the one, Smarty" Shorty stated. "It seems to be glowing. With that, Shorty closed the locket, but stayed on the path. It was twisting, and became so narrow that she could barely fit her body through the ferns. A grayish white mist started to form all around her feet and rose from the ground until she could no longer see her tennis shoes or her toe ring! To her left she noticed a blinking bright fluorescent green sign that read "Nussle Creek Ridge, no vacancy." Well at least she was sure she was still on the right path.

With a little more confidence, Shorty Bean continued down the dense fern path, following the pearl roses. And there it was—the ruby red rose shimmering in all its splendor. It was more vibrant in person then on the map. She lifted her eyes and saw a very large sycamore tree with its branches intertwined into the ground. The leaves on the tree were blowing back and forth, almost like they were swaying and dancing to their own musical song. Shorty looked over her shoulder and behold there was a small wooden door within the tree. Just above the door was an ocean green miniature top hat with a tiny light flickering inside of it. The door was dome-shaped with a little circular window just above it made of woven branches.

"Knock, Knock," Shorty Bean rapped on the door.

"I'm coming!" came a voice from inside and in seconds the door flew open. Shorty blinked with surprise.

"Are you a porcupine?" Shorty asked.

"I'm Ms. Nora! Good day to yaw, Shorty Bean! It is about time. I have me food on the stove and moss in the fire. Now come child and sit, and I will tell you what you need to know," Ms. Nora said as she ushered Shorty Bean inside and motioned for her to sit at the table.

"Don't you have any lights in here?" Shorty asked as she looked around. There was a glow inside, but she couldn't see any lights or where the glow was coming from.

"No, me child, I put peat moss in me fire. Everyone knows peat moss is good for illuminating, plus I have the coin of fire. Well, it is not me real coin of fire, only a replica. But it lights me whole home. You see, the coin has an Irish fable I say, for a man died that day."

"What do you mean?" Shorty Bean asked. "Who died?"

"The great one, me dear. Long ago there was a special place in the land and there was a man known as the "son of the light." A man of which no darkness was in sight. A man that shined as bright as light, who saved us all from doom and gloom and gave us life. He died and rose again you see, to save the world and pardon me. Light, bright, yes, yes, this man of light." Ms. Nora danced and laughed to herself as she spoke the rhyme.

"You have the locket you hold dear. Now open it up and the treasure map will show you my dear. Here is a little help for you on the way," she finished as she pointed at the map. "You are here near the creek of sorts, now journey to the north shore. There you will find the coin that bears a dove."

"I have a riddle for you, how about some toad gum stew? Ha, ha, ha, I laugh with glee, and no one understands this riddle but me." Ms. Nora danced a jig and laughed, patting Shorty Bean's back with her broom. "Good-bye me dear, you must hurry before night fall. Good-bye," Ms. Nora continued to sing and dance. Shorty and Smarty turned to go as Ms. Nora started to sweep the front porch with her broom. She was laughing, singing and dancing as they left her home. As Shorty and Smarty headed toward the coin, they could hear Ms. Nora's voice echoing through the forest.

Chapter Ten

Two Towers of Dixie

The sun began to set signaling that evening was fast approaching. But Shorty Bean had come too far to quit now. She didn't want to go back to the cottage without discovering at least one coin! She opened the locket and just as the scroll had promised, her faith released the treasure map. As it opened, a voice passed through her mind and she heard the words she had seen on the letter. "Seek and you will find."

"Okay, Smarty, onward we go!" Shorty declared with renewed hope.

As they rounded a bend in the path not long after, they came upon a rushing river. The crystal blue water danced and twirled as if it were alive.

"Smarty, this seems like it would be a great time to do some fishing!" As Shorty looked around at all the delightful elements of the forest, the thought struck her that she could make a boat to cruise down the dancing stream.

As the two tread a little further into the forest, they found it was truly full of many delightful things to choose from. There were carrot chairs, tomato tree lights and green rocks that had beds of moss covering over them. But rocks wouldn't work for her boat. Not at all! Then Shorty Bean spotted an enormous zucchini growing deep within the embedded ferns. Now that would work! She climbed up on top of it and jumped up and down on its side until it broke open. Then she began to scrape out all the seeds with her hands to hollow out the skin for a boat. As she threw a handful of the seeds up into the air, they popped like fireworks and disappeared in a burst of

light and color. She jumped at the sound, but then giggled. It was beautiful! She threw large handfuls of seeds into the air and watched the light show of colors they made against the darkening sky. It was like watching fireworks on the fourth of July.

In no time at all the zucchini boat was scooped clean and Shorty Bean and Smarty gently pushed it over to the water's edge. Shorty grabbed a long thin branch from the ground that had fallen from a tree. Next, she took a strand of her long hair and tied it around the branch to make her very own fishing pole. Now, what could she possibly use for a hook? Smarty knew. He pointed to the barrette in her hair. "Yes, that will work," she agreed as she patted his little head. "Thank you, my kind friend."

Smarty smiled at her praise as he climbed back into her backpack. Shorty secured it on her back and then hopped into the zucchini boat. The flowing water immediately caused the boat to drift down the river.

Shorty Bean cast her pole into the water. It was not long before she felt a tug coming from her line. She jerked the line tight and to her delight there was indeed a fish on the end of her barrette hook. As she pulled the fish out of the water, he wiggled ferociously. He didn't look happy at all.

"You must be Sir Davy," Shorty Bean stated.

"Get this hook out of my mouth!" Sir Davy demanded. "What are you trying to do, kill me? Would you like it if a hook was in your mouth?" he asked.

"No, I would not, and I am so sorry," Shorty apologized, but Smarty and I are very hungry and actually we planned to eat you for our supper."

"Eat me, you say? You were going to eat me? I have never heard of such a ridiculous statement in all my life!" he declared as he continued to wiggle even more in her grasp. "Kids, what is wrong with them these days? A fish of my stature and upbringing, I say. Hear, hear, young lady. I am Sir Davy, the commander and chief of Little Dix River." Sir Davy declared with authority. "Shorty Bean, you have come to find the coin of the dove. Is that correct?" he asked.

"Yes, I have," she replied.

"Then keep this boat afloat and I will show you where to find it. You must look over the hill between the two towers of Dixie. Whistle this tune and the ground will shake and the coin that bears a dove will appear for your hands to take." Sir Davy finished the rhyme and then started to whistle, "Triba dee la ta dee, triba do, la da doo. Doo la da, doodle do, do, do." When he finished he squirmed free of Shorty's grasp and dove back into the water. As he swam down the Dix River, he jumped in and out of the water to wave his fins to Shorty and Smarty.

"Well, I guess we've got to find the two towers of Dixie," Shorty Bean commented to Smarty as they headed down the river in the zucchini boat. As they neared the hill Sir Davy had indicated, Shorty noticed a little rock close to shore. She guided the zucchini boat over to it using her fishing pole. The rock gave Smarty and Shorty Bean a way to climb out of the boat and then they pulled it up onto the shore. Smarty's tummy growled, and he began to eat the zucchini boat. He thought it was yummy and if Grandma Ellie was here she would have been so proud that he was eating his vegetables.

Shorty Bean motioned to him, pointing her finger and crossing her thumb over her finger, the signal for "No!"

"Smarty, we may still need our boat. You can't eat it!" She put her hand on the locket and it opened. Then she whistled the tune that Sir Davy had taught her, "Triba dee la ta dee, triba do, la da doo. Doo la da, doodle do, do, do."

As she finished the song, the ground shook and just as Sir Davy had prophesied the coin of the dove appeared!

Shorty Bean scooped it up and gently placed the coin in the locket's chamber. At least they had discovered one of the coins. Suddenly she realized how dark the sky had become. "Hurry Smarty, Grandma and Grandpa will be worried. We need to get back to the cottage!"

Although they seemed to have traveled a long way and Shorty wasn't at all certain which way to go, she noticed the path of hollow ferns which had led them to Ms. Nora's home. They followed the ferns until once again they saw the ruby rose. Shorty breathed a sigh of relief. She knew they were close to the cottage. As they walked past the rose garden, Shorty saw a soft purple glow beaming from the ground where the purple rose had once been. Suddenly, she felt exhausted. She couldn't take another step! "If I can close my eyes for just a moment," she said to Smarty as she lay down and closed her eyes.

To her surprise the voice of her Grandpa woke her up, "I am back! Sorry it took me so long," he apologized.

Shorty rubbed her eyes and looked around trying to remember where she was. Then it all came rushing back to her. "That is okay Grandpa. We just sat here singing songs and looking at the clouds," Shorty Bean told him. She looked at Smarty and winked.

"Are you ready to go in for lunch?" Grandpa asked.

"Yes, we are starving, Grandpa." Shorty expressed. Smarty just nodded his head up and down.

"Come on then," Grandpa said. "Let's head back to the cottage. Your grandma has lunch ready for us."

"Hold on, Grandpa, Smarty needs to walk!" Shorty lifted her little hamdog from her backpack and set him on the ground. "The backpack gets heavy when I have to carry him too long. Plus he needs some exercise," she explained. They all headed back to the cottage together as the roses swayed in the breeze.

Chapter Eleven

The Black Bears

A s they walked past the forest, Grandpa heard a strange noise coming out of the woods.

"Shhh!" he whispered as he held up his hand for them to stop.

Shorty knew what he was thinking. It might be a great black bear of Cantina Village. A branch cracked not far from them followed by a large grunt. There was no time to do anything as large black bears emerged from the woods.

Shorty's heart began to pound. Three sets of piercing red eyes were looking right at them. "Listen to me carefully," Grandpa said. "Don't move. You must keep looking at their eyes! Back up now, real slow, but don't take your eyes off them."

Shorty Bean pulled the locket from her chest and held it up to the black bears. The light that burst from the locket was so bright that her grandpa was blinded for a few moments. So were the bears. The locket's power was unleashed and protected them just as the scroll had promised. As she continued to hold the locket, Shorty Bean felt the powerful force of the chambers. It drained her strength as she continued to hold it high, but she knew she could not drop her arms. With a dreadful roar, the black bears retreated making their way back into the deep woods. It appeared for now, they were safe.

"Grandpa, are you okay?" Shorty Bean asked with a shaky voice.

"What was that? It was like the sun was shining on me so bright that I couldn't see anything. But whatever it was, we are safe now," Grandpa finished.

They walked back to the house on shaky legs as fast as they could.

"What's wrong?" Grandma Ellie asked as soon as she saw them walking up the porch. She had been sitting on the porch petting Mrs. Patty, the blind cat. Grandpa explained to Grandma Ellie what happened.

"You could have been killed," Grandma Ellie declared.

"We almost were!" he nodded. The impact of just how close they had been to that really began to hit home.

"Get inside, both of you" Grandma Ellie insisted. She didn't want to take any chances that the bears might return. Shorty Bean went inside, but ran straight to the

window to look outside one more time. She saw two black ravens flying over the garden path, screeching and crying as they passed by.

"Come away from that window Shorty Bean!" Grandpa shouted. They were all jittery from the experience. Later that night after Grandma Ellie tucked Shorty Bean and Smarty in bed she knelt by the bed, closed her eyes, folded her hands and began to pray. "Night falls and the sky begins to sleep, I pray the Lord your soul to keep. I know that angels will be sitting nearby, to watch you at night and fly, fly, fly. Tuck yourself in bed my dear. And dream of candies and elephant ears. And think about what daybreak will bring, when we spend the day together and watch the morning shine and sing. God bless us everyone; the skies, the oceans, the seasons and the sun. Bless mommies and daddies and little girls too and Smarties and grandpas and grandmas too. And help us to always remember You, You, You. Amen."

Grandma turned the light off and Smarty snuggled very close to Shorty Bean. The smell of lavender floated through the air and the blankets were so warm and soft. In no time at all, Shorty fell fast asleep with little Smarty right at her side.

* * *

The next morning Shorty Bean woke up to the sound of her Grandma's voice as she yelled up the stairs, "Get up child, your mom is on the phone!" Shorty ran downstairs as fast as her legs would carry her. Grandma Ellie handed her the telephone. "Hi, Mom! I miss you so much," Shorty said as she tried to catch her breath from running down the stairs too quickly.

"So, what have you been up to?" her mother began.

Shorty started telling her mom all about the adventures she and Smarty had been on and about the treasure she had found.

"Oh Shorty, you have such a wonderful imagination! Just like I did when I was a little girl," her mother chuckled. "Are you doing ok?"

"Sure Mom, I love it here at Grandma and Grandpa's, but I miss you and Dad and want to come home soon."

"It won't be long before we will all be together again," her mother assured her before they disconnected.

Later that afternoon, Grandma Ellie decided to spend some time with Shorty Bean. She knew her granddaughter like the back of her hand and knew she could use some extra attention after the incident with the bears and after the phone call with her mom. They had a fantastic time together, laughing, holding each other and talking about all sorts of adventurous things. Shorty Bean almost forgot about the black bears and the locket. Almost.

Chapter Twelve

The Kingdom of Ben-Jeer

"I'm going to the woods to see if I can find some toys for Smarty to play with," Shorty called out as she grabbed her jacket and headed for the back door. Maybe she could find a stick or something.

"Now be safe," Grandma said. "And remember to get back home before it gets too dark outside," she finished with a smile and a wave. Shorty waved back to her grandma and grandpa. Grandpa was busy reading the local paper and smoking his cranberry filled pipe as he sat in his green leather chair. She began to hum the melody from his old vinyl record that was playing in the background.

"Hurry back Shorty Bean, and don't be late for dinner," he said again.

Shorty Bean blew Grandpa a kiss. He caught it with his hand and rubbed it on his cheek before Shorty Bean and Smarty ran out back to the pathway. Once outside, she opened the locket and gazed at the treasure map that appeared before her eyes.

"Hmm, it shows we need to travel to Thunder Rail Lake, which is the home of Ben-Jeer the King," Shorty said to Smarty. She had no idea where that was and was thankful for the map. As they walked along the pathway, clouds gathered and covered the sun. It grew extremely cold and dark with the sunlight blocked and then the winds of the north set in. It didn't take long before Shorty Bean was feeling tired, cold and confused.

Suddenly a voice filled the air, "Seek and you will find."

What was happening to her? A shadow overhead startled her. She knew something large had flown over her. But instead of frightening her, it seemed to reassure her and gave an inner strength. Shorty Bean stared down at the treasure map again with renewed strength. She wrapped her coat around her and headed toward the shadow of pines, which according to the map was just over the fields of wild rice. This is where Thunder Rail Lake rested.

Shorty Bean heard thunder all around her, cracking and rolling in the skies. The thunder stopped, and mist filled the air. She could hear a celebration of sorts off in the distance. Then she saw a bridge opening over the lake water.

Voices in unison echoed, "Long live the king." Shorty peered into the mist in the direction of the sound. She could make out the outline of a bridge opening over the lake. That's where the voices were coming from! They grew louder as she neared the bridge and then she heard trumpets along with the voices, "Long live the king!" they continued to shout.

"That sounds like a king of royal descent. Don't you think so, Smarty?"

Smarty nodded his little head as he wiped the condensation that had formed on his aviation goggles with his paws. He cocked his head to listen as bells began to

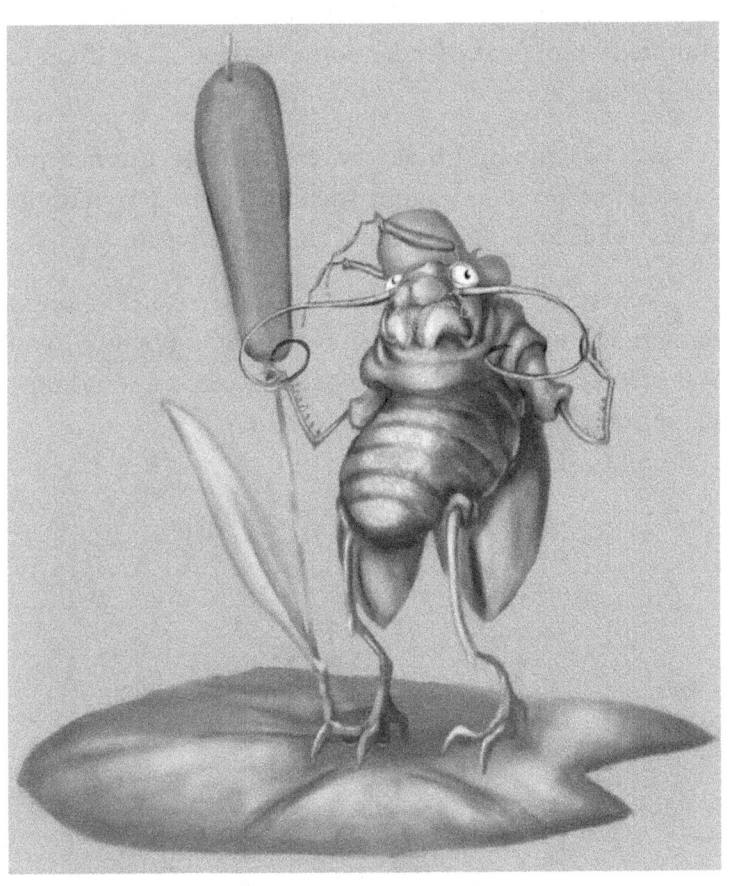

ring. Suddenly there stood before them a vast army of lady bugs! Shorty and Smarty both stopped. Their faces hardly looked friendly. But before they could decide what to do next, a net flew down from the tree and trapped Shorty Bean and Smarty! Lady bug guards quickly surrounded them as the leader commanded, "Take them to see the king at once!"

Shorty Bean and Smarty were taken in the net and carried to a wooden wagon. Then they were driven to the water's edge and placed onto a gigantic lily pad.

"What is happening? Who are you?" Shorty demanded trying to sound brave. Standing before them was a black beetle with a red beret. He had a long mustache and spoke with a French accent.

"Boze of you, off to see za king," he declared as he snapped a willow whip to row them through the water. Shorty might have enjoyed it, if she wasn't shaking so bad for it was an incredible sight to behold. There was a large array of lily pads as far as her eyes could see. The trumpets they heard were lady slipper flowers. And then suddenly before her eyes stood Ben-Jeer the king.

"King Ben-Jeer, we have come to seek the heart coin," Shorty said with a low bow. "Can you help us find where it is?"

"Yes, I can," the king replied in a kind, but authoritative voice. "Open your locket."

As Shorty did, the treasure map reappeared and together they examined it. "Over the hill near the beacon clock tower you must travel," the king instructed. "You must get inside the clock tower house which is made of wood and brick. It won't be easy. You will find a ladder inside a window box. Climb the ladder to reach the top of the clock house tower. Once you get to the top there is door behind the clock where you will find the heart coin that you seek to fill your chamber."

"Thank you so much," Shorty Bean said with another bow. "We will be on our way." As they made their way toward the clock tower, Shorty and Smarty could still hear the lady slippers declaring "Long live the king, long live the king!" until finally it was just a hum in the distance.

Shorty Bean and Smarty left Ben-Jeer's kingdom and traveled towards the beacon tower. The trees were losing

their leaves and the northern winds were becoming stronger. Black ravens hovered over their heads, crying and swooping down towards them. Shorty Bean kept a grasp on the locket that rested around her neck. She could see the clock house tower in the distance, but they had to cross an old weathered log which served as a bridge of sorts first. It was a skinny log, and very long and bumpy. Shorty was apprehensive at first, but slowly started across the log. Little by little she and Smarty made their way, slipping a few times here and there, but always able to regain their balance. As they crossed they could see the clock tower. Shorty kept her eyes on the top of the tall structure as she walked to the door and went inside. Just as the king had instructed, right above the window towards the left was a built-in ladder. Shorty Bean and Smarty climbed the ladder to the second level of the clock tower. They were almost there!

Arriving at the clock door, Shorty reached behind it in search of the coin. Her heart was pounding, but there it was, the heart coin. As Shorty Bean picked it up, the locket door swung open and the heart coin soared into its chamber. Lights flashed and in an instant the locket closed.

Chapter Thirteen

Bow Hunting

Shorty Bean and Smarty had made fast time as they returned from the clock tower, but a quick glance at her watch and she realized they might just be late for dinner. They had no time to waste as they headed back to the cottage. When they reached it, Shorty and Smarty crept through the backdoor and climbed the stairs. Shorty Bean was not hungry anymore. She went into the bathroom, brushed her teeth, changed into her pajamas and then she climbed into bed. Smarty laid his goggles on her dresser, fluffed his cape and dove up onto the bed where he laid his head right on her pillow. They both fell fast asleep. Grandma Ellie shook her head with a smile when she came to check on them for dinner and realized they were already asleep. She quietly left the room and gently closed the door.

The next morning, Shorty Bean got dressed and then devised a plan to sneak outside before Grandma made them breakfast. Her stomach rumbled in protest for they had missed dinner the night before, but she needed the third gold coin of wind and there was no time to lose.

Shorty Bean opened the locket and the treasure map appeared. Tripod, the defender of the box turtles was her next stop according to the map. With Smarty safely tucked away in her backpack, Shorty snuck downstairs, quietly opened the door, lifted her backpack to her shoulder and headed toward the forest. The map led her back down the forest path when she heard a strange swooping sound. At the same time, she felt something fly right through her hair. Without thinking she reached up and grabbed it. Lo and behold, it was a black and orange arrow!

Smarty hunkered down in the backpack shivering, but he managed to pop his head out the side to look at her. "It's ok, Smarty. Don't be afraid," she signed to him.

"Hark, who goes there?" roared a gruff voice.

"It is I, Shorty Bean," she answered.

"Ah yes, that is you. Sorry about the arrow. I have been expecting you," Tripod informed her. A turtle shuffled out to meet Shorty and Smarty. He had a small shell and a strange mechanical leg. Tripod smiled, but then franticly waved his hand. "SSSSSHHHH! Don't' say a word! Do you hear that?" he whispered.

"Hear what?" Shorty Bean asked.

"Listen! SHHHH! Quiet!" Tripod commanded. "I said be quiet! They are here."

"What are you talking about, Tripod?" Shorty inquired.

"Are you crazy? Get down, on the ground now!" he screamed. Shorty Bean, Smarty and Tripod spent the next half hour crawling on their hands, elbows and knees. Not a single word passed between them just in case there were spies in the woods.

Tripod looked from side to side and all around as they made their way forward, but refused to speak until they reached his hut and went inside.

"Oh my, this place is a cluttered mess," Shorty Bean said. There were books and canisters and all sorts of weird stuff. Tripod, they discovered, was a clever scientific character, and he had been working on many explosive science projects. This, in fact, added to his already nervous personality. Shorty reached for a glass bottle.

"Don't touch that!" Tripod yelled at her.

"Okay, geez; can't a little girl look around?" Shorty asked as she pulled her hand back.

Suddenly, a flash of light filled the sky followed immediately by the report of gun shots. "Get down! Get down!" Tripod yelled at the top of his lungs. "INCOMING! INCOMING! Hit the deck!" he screamed as he dove under the wooden table. Tripod held his hands over his head and motioned for Shorty Bean to do the same. Smarty was close behind her. "Listen, Shorty Bean you are not safe here." Tripod told her.

"Tripod, I need your help. Please, will you take Smarty and I to find the coin of wind?"

Tripod nodded, "We will not have to go very far." He reached in his wooden cabinet and pulled out a cobalt glass bottle shaped like a pear. Tripod placed the bottle on the table and told Shorty Bean and Smarty to stand back. He removed the wooden cork from the top of the bottle. In an instant, the glass burst filling the hut with all

the colors of the rainbow. It was a massive show of lights. There before them, twirling in mid-air, was the coin of wind. As had happened with the previous coins, Shorty Bean's locket opened, and the coin of wind fell into its chamber before the locket clicked shut again.

Now, there was only one coin still missing! Shorty Bean could not wait to find it.

"We must go to see White Cloud, the ruler of the forest, the Lord of all," Shorty exclaimed.

"You are right, Shorty Bean. He is the Great Light of the sun that sees and hears everything. He will give you the last coin you seek—the coin of fire" Tripod replied.

"I want to go and see him," Shorty Bean stated.

"Then let us go now," Tripod said. Together they journeyed to the water's edge to the trees of Gazman. The forest grew thick and dark. Shorty shivered as the cold seeped into her body. She felt it pressing on her chest like a dark force was trying to take over her. She folded her arms across her chest and held onto her locket tightly. Her breath formed a white mist flowing out into a cloud each time she exhaled.

They continued down the path through the dense ferns following the brilliant light of the sun that seemed to pierce in and out through the trees. Each time they saw the bright light from the sun, it would give them a supernatural strength to keep going. Finally, the path and the thick woods started to clear…

Chapter Fourteen

White Cloud

The sun shone through the trees as Shorty Bean followed Tripod through the forest. The warmth of the rays felt good and warmed her chilled body as they continued their quest for the last coin.

"What is it?" Shorty Bean asked as Tripod came to an immediate halt. She couldn't make out the expression on his face. It wasn't fear, but it wasn't a smile either. She watched as Tripod removed his head wrap and felt to his knees with his head bowed to the ground. They had found White Cloud.

Shorty Bean squinted in the sunlight as she gazed up into the towering tree that stood taller than any other in the forest. Its branches formed a stairway of sorts that wrapped around the tree as far as she could see up to the sky. That's when she saw him.

His head and face were white, but unlike most eagles, his chest was also white, and his wings were chestnut brown. His broad yellow beak and piercing eyes spoke of authority. This was White Cloud, chief of the eagles.

White Cloud stepped to the edge of his nest located high above the trees as a voice thundered from above, "Shorty Bean, it is I, White Cloud, Lord of all and the protector of the Gazman Forest. I know what was, what is, and what is to come!" he boomed as his words echoed through the forest. "Take off your shoes, for the ground you are standing on is sacred."

"White Cloud, your Majesty," Shorty's voice shook as she bowed her head in reverence. "Very pleased to meet

you." She could feel Smarty quivering within her backpack. He wouldn't even peak his head out the top!

Although a bald eagle, White Cloud also resembled an Indian chief. He had a long white beard and his white chest seem twice as broad as any eagle she had ever seen.

He swooped from the nest and his wings extended so far, she thought they wouldn't clear the trees, but White Cloud glided effortlessly down to where she and Tripod stood. Up close now she noticed he had a retractable gold lens over his right eye that retracted inwards as he gazed at her.

White Cloud spread his wings and wrapped Shorty in an embrace that warmed her entire being. She felt safer than she had ever felt before. "Climb on my back and prepare yourself, for I am going to fly you over and above the clouds of the Gazman Forest," he instructed.

Shorty reached into the backpack and gently reassured Smarty. "Don't be afraid. You will be fine. Obediently, she climbed onto White Clouds strong back. Within seconds they were soaring through the open sky. It was amazing.

"Shorty Bean, look down. What do you see?"

"Those are the trails we have been walking to find the enchanted coins," she realized as she recognized where they were.

"Yes, my dear. I want to show you the hidden places of your journey, where I was watching over you. Although you could not see me, I have been watching over you the

entire time." With that White Cloud soared up through the sky to where dark storms clouds billowed. A misty rain beaded on Shorty's hair, face and clothes and the wind increased in intensity. Shorty could feel the strong muscles of White Clouds back and saw the muscles in his legs bulge out as he flew against the wind. His feathers were spread out like an enormous kite. She could feel his power as their speed increased and he flew them up through the storm and dark clouds to where the sky was once again calm and the clouds billowy and white. Suddenly, they were gliding in peaceful tranquility as they drifted through the air soaring in and out of the clouds. As they did, Shorty Bean saw visions of her journey pass by like pictures in the clouds. There she was at her Grandma and Grandpa's home sitting with them on the porch. And she could see herself walking and laughing with her Grandpa in the rose garden. White Cloud showed her when the black bears came out of the woods. It was the power that he had given the chambers in the locket that had protected her.

In scene after scene, White Cloud showed her that it had been he who had always been there high above the trees, looking down with his gold lens, watching and guiding her. He showed her when the winds of the north became strong and she could barely walk, how he had been the shadow above the darkness that gave her strength. Although she may have felt she was alone, Shorty Bean realized that she had never been alone! White Cloud was always there. She just never saw him.

White Cloud turned to look back at Shorty Bean as they flew and smiled with such compassion and kindness that she felt she would melt. "I have known and cared for you before the beginning of time," he assured her as they continued to pass through the clouds and various scenes from her life.

White Cloud continued to soar through the air until they reached a snow-capped mountain top. Although the temperature was cold, Shorty felt warmed by his presence as she slid off his back with Smarty still in her arms.

"You have done well, my child. Now is the time for you to receive the gold coin of fire," he stated as he lifted his breastplate vest. Underneath was a shining sheath of turquoise and purple beads. White Cloud reached to the center of his chest and nestled in the sheath was a gold coin blazing with fire.

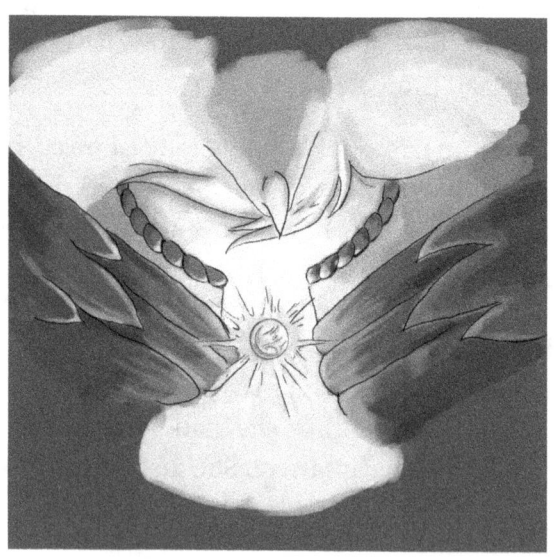

Chapter Fifteen

The Coin of Fire

Shorty turned the coin over in her hand and studied it. This was the same coin that she remembered seeing the replica that illuminated Ms. Nora's tree home at Nussle Ridge Creek. The light that shined from it was as dazzling as the sun. As White Cloud extended the coin to her, the locket on her neck automatically opened as it had before. With his claw, he placed the coin in her hand. Just then, she felt the ground quake beneath her feet and heard rocks breaking from underneath her.

An avalanche!

Large rocks fell from the mountain and plunged into the water beneath her. They had to get to safety. As they began to run, Shorty Bean twisted her ankle and fell. As she did the coin flew from her hand. She watched helplessly as it fell down the mountain. Shorty Bean tumbled down the icy slope as Smarty's cape flapped in the wind.

What happened next all seemed to happen in slow motion as White Cloud effortlessly soared down the side of the mountain until he was just above her. She reached out her hand and suddenly she felt the warmth of his wings, gently pulling her up to safety. He then tucked them safely under the shelter of his wings and Shorty felt comforted and secure. Without a word, he turned and looked at her with piercing eyes. She knew they were safe. White Cloud flew them back up to the mountain and set their feet on the mountain top.

"Do not worry, Smarty," White Cloud spoke gently to the trembling hamdog as he patted him on the head. "You are safe now."

"But what about the coin of fire, White Cloud?" Shorty asked as her face clouded with concern. "It has fallen into the deep river bed,"

"Shorty, you must not know what is to come. It is for another time. It is time for you and Smarty to return. Come back upon my wings, and I will take you back to your Grandpa Andy and Grandma Ellie's cottage."

Shorty Bean, did not understand. Why go back? They had come so far! She had held the last coin in her hand for a brief instant. If she hadn't fallen, the locket would have been complete. And what about the mystery that was to be revealed? She wondered. Was it all lost?

"Do you trust me?" White Cloud asked understanding her thoughts.

"Yes, I do," she said without hesitation. With that she climbed back upon his wings with Smarty in her backpack. White Cloud flew them over the water and over the forest back to her grandparent's cottage. The sun was beginning to set for the evening and a soft dusk was settling over the land.

White Cloud descended near the garden and came to a halt. He reached his wings around Shorty Bean with Smarty in her backpack and deposited them safely onto the ground in front of him.

"Shorty Bean, you must keep the locket close to you at all times until I can return to the Gazman Forest again. Do you trust me?" he asked again.

"Yes, I do," Shorty nodded.

"Then go, and know that I am always with you—always." With that White Cloud flew off back toward the snow-capped mountain. They watched until they could not see him any longer and then ran inside where Grandma Ellie was making dinner. Although it felt like they had been gone for hours, now that they were back home it was almost as if they had never left.

"Did you miss me?" Shorty asked Grandma Ellie.

"Well you were only gone a moment! Were you playing in the garden with Smarty?" she asked.

"Playing in the garden? I was on an adventure," Shorty exclaimed.

"Of course, you were, Shorty Bean," Grandma chuckled. "You always did have an imagination like your mother! Well, come sit down and tell us all about your adventure," Grandma Ellie said as she patted her hand on the sofa for Shorty to come sit beside her and Grandpa Andy.

As she was talking to her grandparents, Shorty's eyes started to close and the sounds in the room faded. Her Grandpa's voice grew faint and she felt her Grandma cover her with a fleece blanket. Nestled in her Grandpa's arms, she fell fast asleep as Grandpa Andy gently stroked her head.

Grandpa scooped Shorty up in his arms and carried her upstairs to bed. Grandma heard Smarty wrestling around in Shorty's backpack. She took him out, gave him some water and some snacks and sent him off to bed too. He was so tired and barely made it up the stairs to her room. He jumped up on the bed and snuggled next to Shorty's pillow.

Voices from downstairs woke Shorty the next morning. She started to turn over and go back to sleep when she realized whose voices they were.

"Mom, Dad!" she screamed. Shorty raced downstairs so fast, she thought she was going to trip and fall.

Both of her parents hugged her tight. "We missed you so, Shorty Bean."

Smarty looked down as Dad patted the top of his head. Smarty's tail was wagging like crazy. Maybe Dad had actually missed Smarty for once. Shorty could only hope!

"Is it time to go home?" Shorty Bean asked.

"Yes, it is," her Dad responded. "Go get your things."

"Come on, honey. I'll help you pack," Grandma told Shorty Bean as they turned to go upstairs.

Chapter Sixteen

Grandma Ellie's Gift

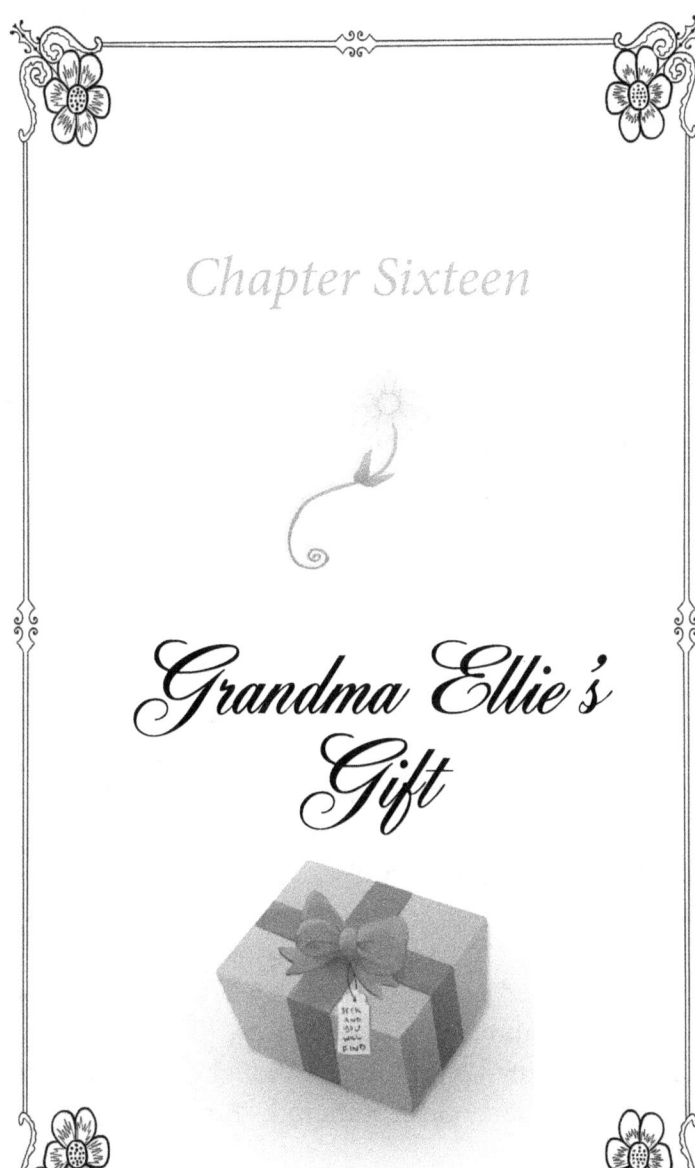

S horty Bean followed her grandma up the stairs to her room. Grandma Ellie took the suitcase and laid it on the bed and started folding her clothes and laying them in neat piles inside the case. As she did she said, "Shorty Bean, I have a present for you."

"Yes, Grandma? What is it?" Shorty asked.

"It is a special gift that I made just for you," she replied with a twinkle in her eyes.

Shorty Bean took the present from her grandmother's outstretched hand. It was wrapped in brown paper with a big red bow. She read the note on the box which said, "Seek and you will find."

She looked up at her Grandma with wonder in her eyes. As she opened the present she saw several patch-work squares that had been hand-sewn. She looked and saw her and Smarty on one of the patches. The next patch was Ms. Nora, the Irish porcupine dancing and laughing as she swept her porch. On another patch was Ben-Jeer's kingdom surrounded by the fields of lady slippers playing trumpets. There were three black bears running away into the woods as the locket was shining bright. There was another patch with Tripod and one of Sir Davy. Shorty's forehead creased as she looked at her Grandma. "How did you know about all my adventures, the animals I met and the enchanted gold coins? I thought that you didn't believe me." Shorty Bean stuttered. "But I, but I, I didn't tell you."

Grandma smiled at her and asked, "Do you trust me? I do believe in you," Grandma said. Just as Grandma Ellie spoke, the loud cry of an eagle filled the sky. Both of them in amazement looked out the window and saw the shadow of his wings fly over the cottage. As he passed the cottage, he tipped his wings towards the bedroom window. Shorty Bean and Grandma both knew it was White Cloud. They smiled and hugged each other tight. Shorty Bean was so glad that her Grandma understood everything without even having to say a word to her.

Shorty grabbed her suitcase, her backpack with Smarty inside and the gift from her grandma and hurried downstairs to where Mom and Dad were waiting to take Shorty Bean and Smarty back home. Everyone said their goodbyes. It was sad for Shorty Bean because she loved her Grandma Ellie and her Grandpa Andy very much. But it was time to go back home to the city.

Shorty Bean climbed into the backseat of the car as Grandma and Grandpa sat on the front porch rocking in their rocking chairs waving to them as they drove away.

Chapter Seventeen

Are We There Yet?

As they were traveling home, Shorty began to daydream as she stared out the car window. All of a sudden, she stopped. "Mom, where did you get that music?" she asked.

"It's an Irish music CD. Do you like it?" Mom asked. "While I was visiting your Aunt Flo, I bought it. I thought it would be a good idea to bring back some of me Irish heritage."

Dad began to belly laugh about the little Irish accent that Mom was trying to pull off as Smarty and Shorty snickered and looked at each other. They weren't laughing about Mom's attempt at an accent. They were laughing because this was the same music that funny ol' Irish-singing porcupine Ms. Nora, had danced to with her broom when Shorty had met her.

Shorty Bean smiled as she looked out the window with her dear old "rat" Smarty on her lap. She couldn't stop thinking about all of the many adventures they had just experienced. She would need to sew some patches on Smarty's cape so that they could remember them all!

The bright Irish tempo was contagious and they all began to sway in their seats with its rhythm. Shorty Bean tapped her toe as she stared down at her daisy toe ring. All the while though, she held the heart locket tightly and wondered when she would complete the mission and find the final coin—the coin of fire.

Already she was looking forward to her next visit with her Grandpa Andy and Grandma Ellie at the cottage again. Maybe it would be during summer break—she could only hope.

The End

About the Author

Holly Szurpicki was born in Detroit, Michigan, the car capital of the world. Although she couldn't drive yet, her imagination had a way of taking her wherever she dreamed to go.

Holly wished one day to be a princess, a park ranger, or an entrepreneur. She states, "Two out of three is not too shabby."

She is passionate about creating stories, screenplays and writing songs. Holly began writing a manuscript in the year 2001 which lay dormant as she focused on raising her two children. But when the year 2008 arrived, she teamed up with a virtual animation studio out of New York. That is when the dream came to life, and the Shorty Bean story became her first novel.

Art and individual creativity have tremendously inspired her throughout her career. Holly possesses visual creativity which takes her to places beyond words to live animation in her mind. Being able to envision her characters and their environments is a true gift, and she recognizes this as supernatural.

Despite many tragic circumstances she has faced throughout her life, Holly has always maintained a positive attitude and loves to encourage others to pursue their God-given dreams.

Her goal for writing children's books is to create a safe and wholesome environment for imagination. Holly desires for children to DREAM BIG, and never forget that there is nothing impossible with God. She believes each one of us has a divine destiny and wants others to never be afraid to pursue their dreams.

Holly lives in northern Minnesota with her husband and two children and a water dog named Klause. She loves the outdoors, photography and fishing to name a few of her passions.

For more information regarding the Shorty Bean series,
future works or general inquiries,
check out her website:
www.hollykszurpicki.com.